EPISODE IV
A NEW HOPE

RYDER WINDHAM

BASED ON THE STORY AND
SCREENPLAY BY
GEORGE LUCAS

ILLUSTRATIONS BY
BRIAN ROOD

EGMONT

We bring stories to life

First published in Great Britain 2015 by Egmont UK Limited
The Yellow Building, 1 Nicholas Road, London W11 4AN

Written by Ryder Windham
Cover Design by Maddox Philpot and Anthony Duke
Illustrated by Brian Rood

© & ™ 2015 Lucasfilm Ltd.
ISBN 978 1 4052 7963 5
61057/1
Printed in China

To find more great *Star Wars* books, visit www.egmont.co.uk/starwars

A LONG TIME AGO IN A GALAXY FAR, FAR AWAY ....

IT IS A PERIOD OF CIVIL WAR. Rebel spaceships, striking from a hidden base, have won their first victory against the evil Galactic Empire.

During the battle, rebel spies managed to steal secret plans to the Empire's ultimate weapon, the Death Star, an armoured space station with enough power to destroy an entire planet.

Pursued by the Empire's sinister agents, Princess Leia races home aboard her starship, custodian of the stolen plans that can save her people and restore freedom to the galaxy ...

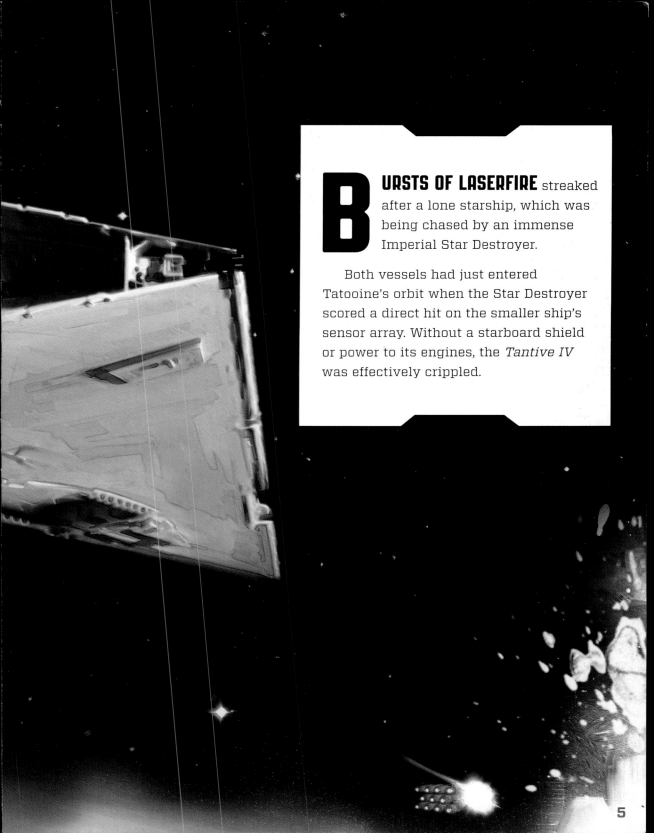

BURSTS OF LASERFIRE streaked after a lone starship, which was being chased by an immense Imperial Star Destroyer.

Both vessels had just entered Tatooine's orbit when the Star Destroyer scored a direct hit on the smaller ship's sensor array. Without a starboard shield or power to its engines, the *Tantive IV* was effectively crippled.

INSIDE THE BATTERED SHIP, C-3PO, a gold-plated humanoid protocol droid; and his counterpart, R2-D2, an astromech, were very worried.

"Did you hear that?" C-3PO said. "They've shut down the main reactor. We'll be destroyed for sure. This is madness!"

Suddenly, sparks blazed at the entry door! The hatch exploded. Before the smoke cleared, white-armoured Imperial stormtroopers charged through, firing their blasters at the rebels. The rebels fought back, and the corridor was filled with deadly, crisscrossing blaster fire.

A **SQUAD OF STORMTROOPERS** secured the corridor, then moved away from the hatch as a tall, caped figure entered. He was clad entirely in black. He was Darth Vader, Lord of the Sith.

Vader surveyed the fallen rebels on the corridor floor. Stepping over the bodies, Darth Vader proceeded into the rebel ship.

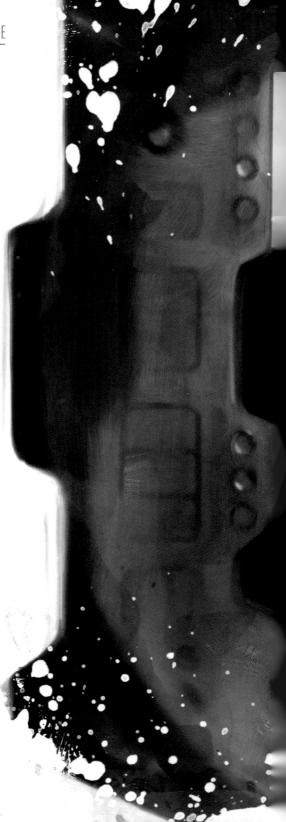

R2-D2 WAS WITH PRINCESS LEIA,

who had called for him. She inserted a data card into a slot beneath R2-D2's radar eye.

From nearby, C-3PO cried, "Artoo, where are you?"

While Leia crept off to hide, R2-D2 moved towards C-3PO's voice.

"At last!" C-3PO said when he saw R2-D2. "Where have you been? They're heading in this direction. What are we going to do? We'll be sent to the spice mines of Kessel or smashed into who knows what!"

R2-D2 rolled away from C-3PO, heading for the escape pod access tunnel.

"Wait a minute," C-3PO said. "Where are you going?"

DARTH VADER and an Imperial officer confronted Princess Leia, who was now a prisoner.

"Darth Vader," Leia said. "Only you could be so bold."

"Don't act so surprised, Your Highness," Vader said. "Several transmissions were beamed to this ship by rebel spies. I want to know what happened to the plans they sent you."

"I don't know what you're talking about," Leia said, feigning innocence. "I'm a member of the Imperial Senate on a diplomatic mission to Alderaan ..."

"You are a part of the Rebel Alliance ... and a traitor," Vader snarled. "Take her away!"

As Vader walked away, Imperial Commander Praji stopped him and said, "Lord Vader, an escape pod was jettisoned during the fighting, but no life-forms were aboard."

Vader said, "She must have hidden the plans in the escape pod. Send a detachment down to retrieve them. See to it personally, Commander. There'll be no one to stop us this time."

C-3PO AND R2-D2 were trudging down a steep dune, leaving behind their life-pod. C-3PO sighed. R2-D2 whistled and made a sharp right turn.

"Where do you think you're going?" C-3PO asked.

R2-D2 answered with a stream of electronic noise.

"Well, I'm not going that way," C-3PO said. "It's much too rocky. This way is much easier."

The astromech uttered more beeps and whistles.

"What mission?" C-3PO said, dumbfounded. "What are you talking about? I've just about had enough of you! Go that way! You'll be malfunctioning within a day, you nearsighted scrap pile!"

When he realised C-3PO was determined to go his own way, R2-D2 turned his dome in the other direction and moved off towards the rocks.

R2-D2 KEPT MOVING. He was on a mission, so he rolled forwards on his treads, proceeding cautiously through a rock canyon.

A pair of lights flickered between two boulders, then winked off. R2-D2 paused. Suddenly, a squat, hooded figure with glowing eyes jumped out from the shadows and fired a blaster at R2-D2! The astromech shrieked as rippling charges of electricity travelled over and through his body. He pitched forwards and crashed against the hard ground.

The Jawa called out to the surrounding shadows, and seven more Jawas scurried from their hiding places. The Jawas picked up R2-D2 and carried the droid to their waiting transport.

A **SQUAD** of Imperial stormtroopers found the abandoned escape pod half buried in the sand.

"Someone was in the pod," the lead trooper said. He raised a pair of macrobinoculars to his helmet's lenses and scanned the desert, then added, "The tracks go off in this direction."

Another stormtrooper bent down to lift a shiny metal disc from the sand. Holding it up for inspection, the stormtrooper said, "Look, sir – droids."

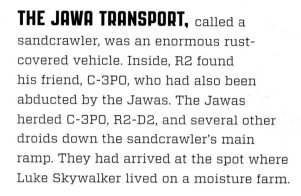

THE JAWA TRANSPORT, called a sandcrawler, was an enormous rust-covered vehicle. Inside, R2 found his friend, C-3PO, who had also been abducted by the Jawas. The Jawas herded C-3PO, R2-D2, and several other droids down the sandcrawler's main ramp. They had arrived at the spot where Luke Skywalker lived on a moisture farm.

He and his Uncle Owen had decided to purchase two droids. The first they chose was C-3PO. The second, a red one, started to come with them – and then exploded!

Turning to the Jawa, Owen said, "What about that blue one? We'll take that one."

C-3PO said, "I'm quite sure you'll be very pleased with that one, sir. He really is in first-class condition. I've worked with him before."

THE DROIDS FOLLOWED LUKE into the moisture farm – their new home. Luke knelt beside R2-D2 and began cleaning him.

"Hello," Luke said to R2-D2.

R2-D2 beeped.

Luke was scraping R2-D2's head carefully with a pick when a fragment broke loose with a snap, and Luke looked up to see a flickering three-dimensional hologram of a young woman being projected from R2-D2's dome. The hologram said, "Help me, Obi-Wan Kenobi. You're my only hope."

"Who is she?" Luke said in awe. "She's beautiful."

C-3PO said, "I'm afraid I'm not quite sure, sir. Artoo says that he's the property of Obi-Wan Kenobi, a resident of these parts. And it's a private message for him."

LUKE LEFT THE GARAGE and crossed the courtyard floor to the dining alcove. He sat down at the table and said, "You know, I think that R2 unit we bought might have been stolen."

Owen glowered. "What makes you think that?"

"Well, I stumbled across a recording while I was cleaning him," Luke said. "He says he belongs to someone called Obi-Wan Kenobi."

Hearing this name, Owen and Luke's aunt, Beru, exchanged nervous glances. Chewing his food thoughtfully, Luke added, "I thought he might have meant old Ben."

"That wizard's just a crazy old man," Owen said.

LUKE STEPPED OUT of the homestead's entrance dome and kicked at the sand. He couldn't stop thinking about Biggs Darklighter, his best friend. He'd seen Biggs just the day before, at the Anchorhead power station. Biggs had returned to Tatooine to tell Luke he'd graduated from the Academy. He'd also confided that he intended to jump ship and join the Rebel Alliance.

Luke stopped to watch Tatooine's giant twin suns set over a distant dune range. The hot wind tugged at his tunic. He felt trapped and longed for adventure.

THE NEXT MORNING Luke's sand-blasted landspeeder raced over the desert. R2-D2 had run away the night before and Luke had to find him - quickly! Luke checked the autoscan on the dashboard's scopes. "Look," he said to C-3PO. "There's a droid on the scanner. Dead ahead. Might be our little R2 unit. Hit the accelerator."

LUKE AND C-3PO found R2-D2 trudging along the floor of a massive canyon. Suddenly, R2-D2 emitted a flurry of frantic whistles and screams.

C-3PO translated: "There are several creatures approaching from the southeast."

"Sand People!" Luke gasped. "Or worse!"

Luke climbed a ridge to get a better look but was ambushed by a hidden Sand Person. Three Sand People hauled Luke's unconscious body down to the canyon floor and dumped him beside some rocks; then they began to strip the vehicle, tossing parts and supplies in all directions.

But when a great howling moan echoed through the canyon, the three Sand People fled from the scene. An old man appeared. Luke stirred and his eyes widened. "Ben? Ben Kenobi?"

THE OLD MAN was indeed Obi-Wan (Ben) Kenobi. His house was a dome-roofed hovel. Inside, Obi-Wan explained to Luke, "I was once a Jedi Knight, the same as your father." He removed a shiny object from a trunk. "Your father wanted you to have this when you were old enough, but your uncle wouldn't allow it."

Luke asked, "What is it?"

"Your father's lightsaber," Ben said. "This is the weapon of a Jedi Knight."

Luke asked, "How did my father die?"

Obi-Wan said, "A young Jedi named Darth Vader helped the Empire hunt down and destroy the Jedi Knights. He betrayed and murdered your father."

As Ben touched R2-D2's dome, his hologram projector flicked on.

"General Kenobi," said Princess Leia's hologram, "years ago you served my father in the Clone Wars. Now he begs you to help him in his struggle against the Empire. I have placed information vital to the survival of the Rebellion into the memory systems of this Artoo unit. You must see this droid safely delivered to him on Alderaan. Help me, Obi-Wan Kenobi. You're my only hope."

Ben looked at Luke and said, "You must learn the ways of the Force if you're to come with me to Alderaan."

DARTH VADER travelled by Star Destroyer to deliver Princess Leia Organa to the Death Star.

"Until this battle station is fully operational, we are vulnerable," said Commander Tagge. "The Rebel Alliance is more dangerous than you realise."

Admiral Motti sneered, "Dangerous to your starfleet, Commander – not to this battle station!"

"If the rebels have obtained a complete technical readout of this station," countered Tagge, "it is possible, however unlikely, that they might find a weakness and exploit it."

From beside Grand Moff Tarkin, Darth Vader said, "The plans you refer to will soon be back in our hands."

When Motti mocked Vader and the Force, the Sith Lord used the Force to choke him until Tarkin ordered Vader to release him.

"This bickering is pointless," Tarkin said. "Lord Vader will provide us with the location of the rebel fortress by the time this station is operational. We will then crush the Rebellion with one swift stroke."

LUKE, BEN AND THE TWO DROIDS were speeding across Tatooine when they came upon what was left of the Jawa sandcrawler. Dozens of Jawas lay dead, their small forms scattered across the sand.

Luke said, "These are the same Jawas that sold us the droids."

Ben pointed out that only Imperial stormtroopers were so precise in their attacks. An awful realisation hit Luke: "If they traced the robots here, they may have learned who they sold them to, and that would lead them back … home!"

Luke jumped into the landspeeder and sped away from the burning sandcrawler. He saw the rising smoke from kilometres away. The Lars homestead was consumed by a fiery blaze. His aunt and uncle were dead. There was nothing left for Luke on Tatooine. He told Ben that he would go with him to Alderaan.

ON THE DEATH

Star, Darth Vader interrogated Princess Leia. "And now, Your Highness, we will discuss the location of your hidden rebel base."

There was an electronic hum from behind Vader; then a spherical black droid hovered slowly into the cell. It was an interrogator droid. Leia's eyes widened with fear. The droid extended its syringe and hovered towards her.

The cell door slammed and the interrogation began.

APPROACHING MOS EISLEY

spaceport, Luke slowed the landspeeder. Suddenly, five white-armoured stormtroopers noticed C-3PO and R2-D2.

The squad leader said, "Let me see your identification."

"You don't need to see his identification," Ben said, using the Force.

Looking at his fellow stormtroopers, the squad leader said, "We don't need to see his identification."

Ben said, "These aren't the droids you're looking for."

"These aren't the droids we're looking for," the squad leader repeated, and waved them through.

Luke drove the landspeeder away from the stormtroopers.

"I'M READY FOR ANYTHING," Luke said as he followed Ben into the cantina. They were looking for a ship to take them to Alderaan.

The bartender was scowling at Luke when an alien spat out, "Negola dewaghi wooldugger!"

A disfigured man said, "He doesn't like you."

Ben said calmly, "This little one's not worth the effort. Come, let me get you something."

The man with the disfigured face suddenly flung Luke away from the bar. Luke crashed into a nearby table, and his attackers reached for their blaster pistols.

Ben drew his lightsaber. The blade flashed on and swept past the blaster-wielding criminals. The disfigured man had a deep slash across his chest. The alien screamed and his right arm fell to the floor, still clutching its blaster.

The entire fight had lasted only seconds.

BEN NODDED at a gigantic furry Wookiee and said to Luke, "Chewbacca here is first mate on a ship that might suit us."

Chewbacca sat down with them in a private booth. They were soon joined by Han Solo, who said, "I'm captain of the *Millennium Falcon*. Chewie here tells me you're looking for passage to the Alderaan system."

"Yes, indeed," Ben said. "If it's a fast ship."

"Fast ship?" Han said. "You've never heard of the *Millennium Falcon*? I've outrun Imperial starships. She's fast enough for you, old man."

After payment was agreed upon, Han said, "OK. You guys got yourselves a ship. Docking Bay Ninety-four."

NSIDE DOCKING BAY 94 were a number of gangsters and at least one bounty hunter.

"Solo," Jabba the Hutt bellowed at the *Falcon*. "Come out of there, Solo!"

"Right here, Jabba," Han called from behind the Hutt. "I've been waiting for you."

Jabba wanted Han to pay back money for a smuggling job that had failed.

"Look, Jabba. Even I get boarded sometimes," Solo said. "You think I had a choice? I'll pay you back plus a little extra. I just need a little more time."

Jabba said, "Han, my boy, you're the best. But if you fail me again, I'll put a price on your head so big you won't be able to go near a civilised system."

Chewbacca followed Han into the *Falcon*.

PRINCESS LEIA was brought to the control room of the Death Star.

"Governor Tarkin," Leia said. "I recognised your foul stench when I was brought on board."

Tarkin smiled. "Charming to the last. Princess Leia, before your execution I would like you to be my guest at a ceremony that will make this battle station operational. No star system will dare oppose the Emperor now."

She said, "The more you tighten your grip, Tarkin, the more star systems will slip through your fingers."

"Not after we demonstrate the power of this station," Tarkin informed her with confidence. "Since you are reluctant to provide us with the location of the rebel base, I have chosen to test this station's destructive power ... on your home planet of Alderaan."

Leia begged Tarkin to spare her peaceful planet, but he did not listen. In one explosive instant, Alderaan was gone.

IN THE *MILLENNIUM FALCON'S* hold, Luke was testing his lightsaber skills against a remote. His eyes followed the remote, but his movements were stiff.

Ben placed a helmet over Luke's head and lowered the blast shield so it covered his eyes. "This time, let go of your conscious self and act on instinct."

Luke laughed. "I can't even see. How am I supposed to fight?"

"Your eyes can deceive you," Ben said. "Don't trust them."

Luke relaxed and … somehow, he sensed the remote's movements. The remote fired three bursts and Luke blocked each shot.

"That's good," Ben told him. "You have taken your first step into a larger world."

THE *FALCON* dropped out of hyperspace into realspace.

Han said, "Our position is correct, except … no Alderaan! It ain't there. It's been totally blown away."

"What? How?" Luke asked.

"Destroyed … by the Empire!" Ben said.

An alarm sounded and Han glanced at a sensor scope. An Imperial TIE fighter streaked past the *Falcon*.

"If they identify us, we're in big trouble," Luke said.

Han said, "Chewie – jam its transmissions."

"Look at him," Luke said. "He's heading for that small moon."

"That's no moon! It's a space station," Ben said.

The *Falcon* began to shake violently. "We're caught in a tractor beam!" Han explained. "It's pulling us in."

TARKIN AND DARTH VADER

were in the Death Star conference room when an intercom buzzed. An officer announced, "We've captured a freighter. Its markings match those of a ship that blasted its way out of Mos Eisley."

Vader said, "They must be trying to return the stolen plans to the princess. She may yet be of some use to us."

As Vader entered the hangar, an officer said, "There's no one on board, sir. According to the log, the crew abandoned ship right after takeoff."

"Send a scanning crew aboard," Vader ordered. "I want every part of the ship checked."

Then Vader said to himself, "I sense something ... a presence I've not felt since ..."

Then it hit him.

Obi-Wan Kenobi.

NSIDE THE *FALCON*, Luke, Han and the others emerged from their hiding place. Then the group split up. Obi-Wan went to turn off the tractor beam so they could leave. The droids stayed near the hangar, while Han, Luke and Chewie decided to rescue the princess.

In stormtrooper disguises, Luke and Han escorted Chewbacca through a Death Star corridor. The lift door opened and they stepped in. Han pressed the button for level five and said, "This is not going to work."

"Why didn't you say so before?" Luke said.

"I *did* say so before!" Han protested.

ON THE DETENTION LEVEL, Chewbacca roared and lashed out, smashing a guard. Then Han and Luke blasted the other Imperial troops. Han scanned a data screen. "Here it is ... twenty-one eighty-seven. You go and get the princess. I'll hold them here."

Luke ran up the steps and entered the corridor. He slapped a button on the wall and the cell door slid up. Princess Leia was sleeping. She opened her eyes and said, "Aren't you a little short for a stormtrooper?"

"Huh?" Luke replied. "Oh ... the uniform." He pulled off his helmet. "I'm Luke Skywalker. I'm here to rescue you. I've got your R2 unit. I'm here with Ben Kenobi."

"Ben Kenobi!" Leia cried, jumping up. "Where is he?"

Luke said, "Come on!"

"IT COULD BE WORSE.
TRY AND BRACE IT WITH
SOMETHING!"

TO ESCAPE the other stormtroopers, Han, Leia, Luke, and Chewie jumped into a garbage chute. They landed in a deep pile of trash.

"It could be worse," Leia said.

The walls rumbled and suddenly pushed inwards. It was worse.

Leia said to Han, "Try and brace it with something!"

"Wait a minute!" Luke cried, and reached for his comlink transmitter. "See-Threepio. Come in, See-Threepio!"

C-3PO said into the transmitter, "We've had some problems—"

Luke interrupted. "Shut down all the garbage mashers on the detention level!"

At the last moment, the walls stopped. R2-D2 had plugged into the main computer and told it to stop them. The little droid had saved the day!

AFTER GETTING OUT of the trash compactor, Han and Luke removed their stormtrooper armour. They walked down a hallway; then, as the group rounded a corner, they ran straight into several approaching stormtroopers.

"It's them!" shouted the squad leader. "Blast them!"

Han fired and charged the startled troopers, who turned and ran back up the hallway. As Han chased and fired at the troopers, he shouted to his friends, "Get back to the ship!"

LUKE AND LEIA were spotted by yet another squad of stormtroopers. They raced up a ramp and were through a doorway before they realised the floor ended at an enormous air shaft.

"I think we took a wrong turn," Luke said.

Across the chasm, another open doorway beckoned them. Blaster fire exploded behind them. Leia hit a switch and the door slid shut. While she fended off more troopers, who were shooting at them from above, Luke pulled a grappling hook from his belt. He tossed the hook high and it whipped around a pipe.

Leia kissed Luke's cheek and said, "For luck!"

They swung across the abyss and landed on the opposite ledge.

HAN AND CHEWBACCA raced through a corridor with many stormtroopers hot on their trail. They ran into the hangar and saw the *Falcon* with its landing ramp still down.

"Didn't we just leave this party?" Han said. He then saw Leia and Luke rushing up from the other end of the hallway. "What kept you?" he said.

"We ran into some old friends," Leia joked, catching her breath.

Luke asked, "Is the ship all right?"

"Seems OK, if we can get to it," Han answered. "Just hope the old man got the tractor beam out of commission."

Inside the hangar, C-3PO turned to R2-D2 and said, "Come on, Artoo, we're going!"

Then everyone ran for the *Falcon*'s landing ramp.

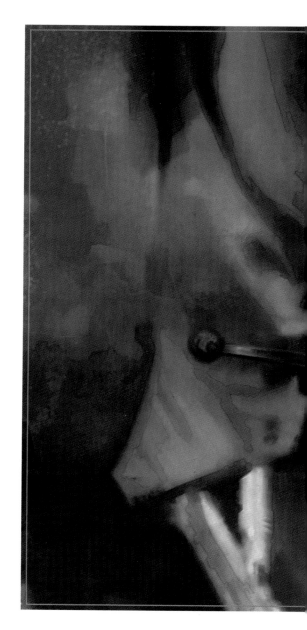

AT THE END of a tunnel leading to the hangar, Ben saw a tall, shadowy form. It was his former apprentice, Darth Vader.

"I've been waiting for you, Obi-Wan," Vader said. "The circle is now complete. When I left you, I was but the learner; now I am the master."

"Only a master of evil, Darth," Obi-Wan said.

There was a loud electric crackle as their lightsabers made contact.

"You can't win, Darth," Obi-Wan said. "If you strike me down, I shall become more powerful than you can possibly imagine."

"Ben?" Luke asked as he came to a stop by the *Falcon*.

Ben looked at Luke and smiled; then he raised his lightsaber before him and closed his eyes. Vader's lightsaber swept through the air. Ben's cloak and lightsaber fell to the floor – but his body was gone.

From nowhere, Luke heard Ben's voice: "Run, Luke! Run!"

WITH LUKE AND THE OTHERS on board, the *Falcon* blasted away from the Death Star. In the main hold, Leia sat by Luke. He shook his head sadly and said, "I can't believe he's gone."

Han rushed into the hold. Looking at Luke, he said, "Come on, buddy, we're not out of this yet!"

Luke followed Han to the gunport turrets. The *Falcon* shuddered as its shields took a laser hit from one of the four TIE fighters.

Han tracked one fighter and fired with his laser cannon, but missed. He got another TIE fighter in his sights and blasted laserbolts at it. The TIE fighter exploded. Luke swung the cannon and scored a direct hit. Another TIE fighter zoomed towards the *Falcon*, but Luke fired back and took that one out too. The last TIE fighter zoomed in. Han swivelled behind his laser cannon, and the ship was consumed in a fiery explosion.

Luke laughed. "That's it! We did it!"

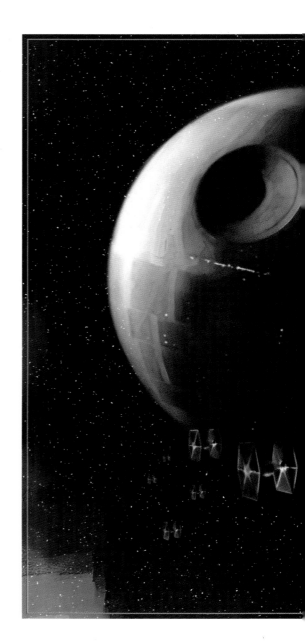

THE DEATH STAR followed the *Falcon* to Yavin 4. It was preparing to blow up the rebel base as soon as it was within range. Meanwhile, all the rebels had gathered to see if there was a way they could blow up the Death Star first.

"Its defences are designed around a direct large-scale assault," General Dodonna said. "A small one-man fighter should be able to penetrate the outer defence. An analysis of the plans provided by Princess Leia has demonstrated a weakness in the battle station."

R2-D2 beeped proudly.

"The target area is only two metres wide," Dodonna continued. "It's a small thermal exhaust port. A precise hit will start a chain reaction which should destroy the station."

A few minutes later, Luke climbed up the ladder to his X-wing.

HAN SOLO had to leave to pay Jabba the money he owed him. The X-wing and Y-wing starfighters sped away across space. Luke was flying low over the Death Star's surface when he heard Ben's voice again: "Luke, trust your feelings."

The battle was hard-fought. Soon, only Luke and a few other rebel pilots were still alive. He said to the others, "We're going in full throttle. That ought to keep those fighters off our back."

They followed Luke into the Death Star trench, where Imperial cannons opened fire.

Then Vader and the TIE fighters arrived.

"I'M ON THE LEADER," Darth Vader told his wingmen.

The three TIE fighters sped after the lone X-wing that remained.

Luke adjusted the lens on his targeting scope. Just then, he heard Ben's voice: "Use the Force, Luke."

Darth Vader sensed the change. He said, "The Force is strong in this one!"

Suddenly, an unexpected blast of laserfire struck one of the TIE fighters. It exploded. Vader exclaimed, "What?" He glanced up.

It was the *Millennium Falcon*.

"Yahoo!" Han Solo hollered as he descended rapidly.

The *Falcon* raced toward the TIE fighters. Vader's wingman panicked and collided with Vader's TIE fighter before crashing into the side wall of the trench.

Vader fought to regain control of his fighter, but it continued to tumble across space.

LUKE LOOKED UP AND SMILED, then concentrated on the exhaust port. He looked at his targeting scope.

Ben's voice said, "Luke, trust me."

Luke reached towards his control panel and pressed a button. The targeting scope retracted and moved away from his helmet. Luke's action was detected by the controllers at the rebel base. A controller announced, "His computer's off." Addressing Luke directly, he said, "You switched off your targeting computer. What's wrong?"

"Nothing," Luke answered as he stayed on course for his target. "I'm all right."

He fired.

THE THREE SURVIVING REBEL STARFIGHTERS and the *Falcon* were barely out of the danger zone when the Death Star exploded in an immense, blinding flash.

"Great shot, kid," Han said into his comm. "That was one in a million."

Luke let out a deep breath and relaxed. Ben's voice said, "Remember, the Force will be with you … always."

Luke smiled all the way back to Yavin 4.

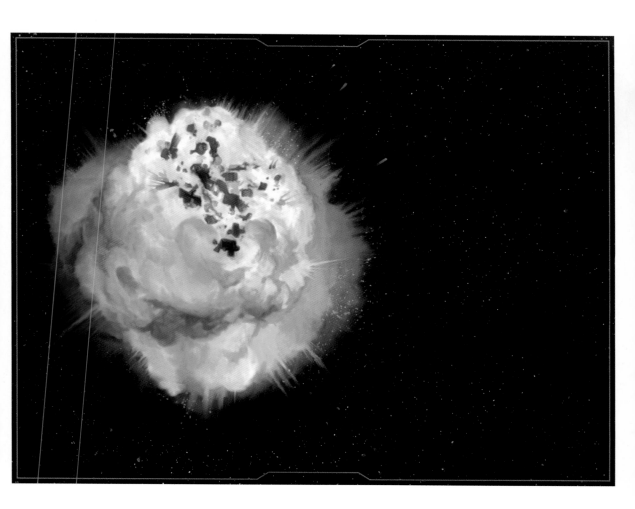

N THE EXPANSIVE RUINS of the temple's throne room, hundreds of uniformed rebel troops stood at attention. Luke, Han and Chewbacca entered. When the trio arrived at the steps of the dais, the troops turned simultaneously on their heels to face the rebel leaders. Han bowed as Leia placed a medallion around his neck.

Luke glanced at C-3PO, who stood beside the rebel leaders. A happy beeping sound came from R2-D2. Leia placed a medallion around Luke's neck, too.

The ancient temple was suddenly filled with loud cheers and applause.

The battle against the Empire was far from over, but a small band of heroes had destroyed the Death Star – and won a great victory for the rebels!

MAY THE FORCE BE WITH YOU!